THIS CANDLEWICK BOOK BELONGS TO:

_____

_____

_____

For the Radner family — Amanda, Emily, Allen,
and Dawn — with big love

Special thanks to Scott Magoon, Monica Perez, James R. Hesse of the Justice
Department, Jill Marsal, and the inimitable Sandra Dijkstra

First paperback edition 2008

The Library of Congress has cataloged the hardcover edition as follows:
Yang, Belle.
Hannah is my name / Belle Yang. — 1st ed.
p. cm.
Summary: A young Chinese girl and her parents emigrate to the
United States and try their best to assimilate into their San Francisco
neighborhood while anxiously awaiting the arrival of their green cards.
ISBN 978-0-7636-2223-7 (hardcover)
1. Chinese Americans — Juvenile fiction. [1. Chinese Americans — Fiction.
2. Immigrants — Fiction. 3. San Francisco (Calif.) — Fiction.] I. Title.
PZ7.Y1925Han 2004
[E] — dc22   2003069675

ISBN 978-0-7636-3521-3 (paperback)

2 4 6 8 10 9 7 5 3 1

Printed in China

This book was typeset in Golden Cockerel ITC.
The illustrations were done in gouache.

Candlewick Press
2067 Massachusetts Avenue
Cambridge, Massachusetts 02140

visit us at www.candlewick.com

Hannah Is My Name

Belle Yang

CANDLEWICK PRESS
CAMBRIDGE, MASSACHUSETTS

Hannah is my name in this new country. It doesn't sound at all like my Chinese name, Na-Li, which means *beautiful*.

Hannah is spelled the same backward. Mama and Baba think it's easy to learn because I don't know English yet.

It feels strange to become Hannah all of a sudden.

At home they just call me Tadpole. I like that. Tadpoles are spunky and have a long way to grow, just like me.

I used to catch tadpoles in the rice paddy and put them in a jar to watch them grow into frogs. That's when we lived in Taiwan, an island off the coast of China. There, bamboo plants grow taller than the houses with their grass roofs.

We came to America by airplane over the ocean, and we want to stay and make this country our home. But it is not easy to become an American if you are not born here.

When we are Americans, Baba says we will be free to say what we think. An American girl is free to be anything she chooses, says Mama. We want to become Americans more than anything in the world. We want to be free.

The first thing we have to do is find a place to live that doesn't cost much. Our first home in America, 636 Bush Street, is a skinny building like a lime Popsicle.

It's in the middle of a hilly city called San Francisco. The rules say no children in the building. But when Jewel, the manager, sees us, she says, "Hmm, a little girl, huh? Well, just as long as she is quiet and doesn't jump up and down and disturb the folks down below."

Her green eyes twinkle behind pointy glasses that tilt up. They look like cats' eyes. I hide behind Mama to show her how nice and small I can be.

I like it here at 636 Bush Street. The elevator looks like a lion's cage, and we take it all the way up to the fifth floor. Our living room becomes the bedroom at night when Baba and Mama's bed pulls from the wall. I sleep on the sofa, but I have a desk of my very own, where I learn my ABCs.

To become Americans, we must go to Chinatown and see Mr. Choo. He helps people new to the country fill out papers with lots of questions, like where did you work and where did you go to school in the old country?

Mama answers in Chinese, and Mr. Choo writes it down in English.

When it is all done, Mr. Choo tells Mama, "Take these papers to the immigration office. Pay them a fee. After that, there is nothing left to do but wait. If the government mails you green cards, one for each of you, it means you can stay in America. But the green cards may never come if the government does not believe you are honest."

"Can't we make them with scissors and my green crayons?" I ask.

"No, little one, it's not that easy!" Mr. Choo says. It is the first time I hear him laugh.

Mama looks worried when we leave.

Without the green cards, Mama and Baba are not supposed to have jobs. Mama was fired from the store where she sewed buttons and labels on clothes all day because the owner found out she didn't have a green card. She cried so hard, I could only pet her hair. "Don't worry, Mama," I told her. "I don't need toys or new shoes."

Mama looked at the empty milk bottle on the table. "Tadpole, it's just that I don't want you to grow up hungry, like Baba and I did," she said.

Mr. Goodman at the hotel hired Baba because he liked Baba's honest face. He likes Baba even more now because Baba saved the hotel from burning down when a guest fell asleep in his bed with a cigarette. Baba saved the man's life!

"Just be careful on the job," Mr. Goodman told Baba. "Sometimes inspectors will make a surprise visit to make sure our workers have green cards. If they catch you, they can send you and your family back to Taiwan. I'll get in trouble, too."

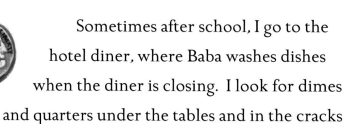

Sometimes after school, I go to the hotel diner, where Baba washes dishes when the diner is closing. I look for dimes and quarters under the tables and in the cracks of the orange plastic seats, but mostly I find gum of all colors stuck underneath. On days when I can't find even a penny, Baba puts a dime in the middle of the floor when I'm not looking. I know he's doing it, but I pretend to be surprised because I don't want him to be disappointed.

One day a big man in a uniform and cap comes and peeks in through the glass door. "Baba," I cry, "is he looking for the green cards?"

Baba only laughs and pulls my braid. "Don't worry, Tadpole. He's the doorman. He's only making sure you're not eating too much ice cream."

Still, I don't trust this man in uniform.

When it is dark outside, Baba and I walk home together, but we stop first at the big Woolworth's store on the corner of Market Street, where the cable cars go *ding-ding-ding* and turn around. They sell practically everything, even parakeets in golden cages. While Baba looks at the magazines, I read *Curious George*.

When it's time to go, Baba asks, "Is that enough, Tadpole?"

I nod and try not to look disappointed. I put the book back on the shelf. We head up the hill to 636 Bush Street, my hand in his big hand. The shoes he bought at the secondhand store are coming apart, their wide hungry mouths going *slap-slap-slap* on the pavement.

Baba says when the green cards come, he will find work that does not wear him out so much. "It will be a job that pays more," he says, "and when that happens, I'll buy you your very own books."

As we walk past Union Square, we hear a guitar and voices singing, "This land is your land, this land is my land. . . ." I hum along because I am learning this song at school.

Bb Cc Dd Ee Ff Gg Hh Ii Jj Kk
Martin Luther King Jr.
1929 - 1968
LIFE
Sara
Hannah
Joe

At Commodore Stockton School, I am in the first grade. I am learning English. I'm scolded by the teacher for talking in class. But it's better than not being able to talk at all. I'm not lonely anymore, like on the first day when I could only say, "Hannah is my name."

I also understand the teacher much better. One morning she cried when she told us a great man had just been killed.

His name was Martin Luther King. "He wanted all people to be treated fairly," she said, "whatever the color of their skin."

Mr. King must have been fighting for my family to be treated kindly too. Baba and Mama say this is why we came to America.

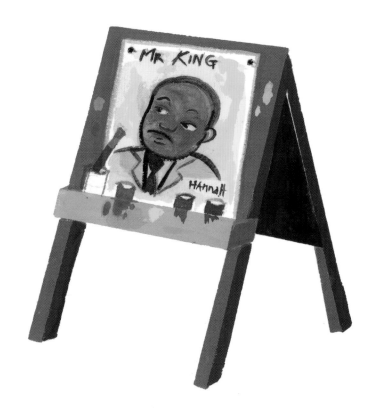

I love school, but I worry a lot when I am there. Yesterday was my friend Janie's last day. Her whole family was told to go back to Hong Kong. They caught her father working at a Chinese restaurant. He had no green card. I gave Janie my bracelet. It has *Hannah* spelled in alphabet beads so she will remember me always. She gave me her pink rabbit's foot.

"I hope it will bring you lots of luck," she said.

Now that she's gone, sometimes it feels like there is a big hole inside my chest. I stroke the rabbit's foot whenever I feel lonely.

On some days when school lets out, Mama and I walk to Chinatown, where we buy bamboo shoots, snow peas, and tofu. I don't like looking at the ducks hanging in the shops, but I like the moon cakes filled with sweet beans at the bakery. Mama takes one handle of the shopping bag and I take the other because it is too heavy for her to carry by herself.

When we get home, the first thing we do is to check the mailbox. All day long our hope stretches out like a rubber band. It snaps back when the green cards are not there.

When Baba comes home to 636 Bush Street in the evening, Mama does not say, "Still no green cards," but her quiet look tells him so.

Soon I am in the second grade, but still the green cards have not come.

At the diner, I do math while Baba sweeps the floor. One afternoon, there is a *rat-tat-tat* on the glass door, and my heart jumps like a frog inside my chest. It's the man in the uniform, and he is wearing a terrible face. He pushes the door open, grabs Baba's arms, and points at me. I want to bite his leg to make him stop shaking poor Baba.

"They're here to check for green cards!" he says. *"Come with me. I'll show you a way to get out — down the freight elevator and then out the back!* Quick!*"*

Baba and I do as he tells us. As the door closes, we hear many footsteps. The man in the uniform says to someone, "Nobody down there but some mighty hungry rats."

Baba throws his apron down on some crates as we dash out the back door and into the alley. We stop running only when we are out of breath.

After that day, I go with Baba to thank the man in uniform. That is when Baba asks Mr. Goodman for work at night, when the front door of the diner is all locked up. Now Baba comes home when the birds are just opening their eyes. I can almost hear his achy bones complain *aiyo* when he tumbles into bed. "When will the green cards ever come?" he sighs.

I want to tell him, "Soon, Baba. Very soon," but I worry, too.

We have been waiting so long, I have grown another two inches.

One day when I come home from school, I find Baba snapping his fingers and humming a song. He says he is not working tonight. Mama does not scold me when she hears the *squish* of my shoes, wet from playing in the fountain at Huntington Park. And I smell pot stickers, dumplings filled with cabbage and meat that we eat on special occasions. They are sizzling in the pan. They are even better than the French fries with ketchup that Mr. Yee sells on Stockton Street.

Mama smiles like a daisy. She says, "That's for you, Tadpole," as she points to a package tied with a ribbon. I unwrap it and find my very own book. Inside the cover is a small piece of paper. It is pale blue, not jade green like I expected. I think they should have called it a blue card, but maybe they just ran out of green paper this year.

But I don't care, because it is the most beautiful thing I have ever seen. It has my name printed importantly on it. Not Tadpole, but Hannah Lin.

Suddenly all the clouds are gone. We don't have to stay quiet and make ourselves small.

Hannah Lin, I repeat to myself. Hannah doesn't sound like a stranger's name anymore. It's my name. Hannah is my name.

And America is our home.

Belle Yang was born in 1960 in Taiwan and came to the United States with her parents at the age of seven. She has studied at the Pasadena Art Center College of Design and the Beijing Institute of Traditional Chinese Painting. She has had solo museum shows and has written and illustrated two highly praised adult books and a picture book. She says, "*Hannah Is My Name* is based on our first years in San Francisco. We arrived in the fall of 1967 via Japan. I missed my old friends and teacher, but it was not a miserable yearning. It was a great privilege to come to the United States, and we didn't look back." This is Belle Yang's first book with Candlewick Press.